Rooster Wore Skinny Jeans

Written by
Jessie Miller

Illustrated by
Barbara Bakos

On a typical Wednesday at **Rosemary Mill**,
A countryside farm run by old Farmer Phil,

The rooster was making his rounds in the coop,

When a brown paper package arrived on the stoop.

He thought, "There's no way! It's too soon! It can't be!
I just ordered them Monday... the shipping was free!"
He eagerly tip-toed his way to the door,
Then bent down to pick up his box from the floor.

He tore off the tape with a **big** cheesy grin,
Then marvelled in awe at the contents within.

The sparkling **stitching**, a **striking gold** hue!

The indigo **denim**, a **dazzling** blue!

"The **flattering** rise and the **slimming** design,
Not too loose, not too snug... these jeans are **divine!**"

He went through the farm with a confident stride.

He felt like a **king**. He had nothing to hide!

"The others will love the new jeans that I've bought!"

Their reaction, however, was not what he'd thought.

At first there were **stares**, a few **snickers**, a leer.
Then the crow taunted loudly for others to hear.

They **howled** in laughter and whistled his name,
As the rooster ran off, his face burning with shame.

He hid in the barn on a tall bale of hay,
Hoping the others would just go away.

He caught a quick glance of himself from behind,
And suddenly **everything** cleared in his mind.

"What's not to love? Are they being **sarcastic**?
These jeans are amazing; my bum looks fantastic!"

He calmed himself down, let the bad feelings sink,
Then he thought, "You know what? **I don't care** what they think!

I wanted these jeans, and I bought them for **me**.

Their opinions don't matter. I'll show them! They'll see!"

He flew to the top of the barn in a streak,
Stood as tall as he could on the uppermost peak.

Cock a doodle doo !

He brushed off all feelings of **worry** and **doubt**,
Then he **cockled** and **doodled** and **dooed** with a shout!

A chicken spoke out with her head towards the sky,
"I kind of **admire** the nerve of that guy...
He won't be held back by the things that we say,
He is being **himself**, and I think that's okay."

The animals **cheered** and encouraged his call,
And the rooster, he **beamed** at the sight of it all.

Later that night, as the farm lay to rest,
The rooster pre-ordered a **gold sequined vest.**

Rooster Wore Skinny Jeans
An original concept by author Jessie Miller
© Jessie Miller
Illustrated by Barbara Bakos

MAVERICK ARTS PUBLISHING LTD
Studio 3A, City Business Centre, 6 Brighton Road, Horsham, West Sussex, RH13 5BB
© Maverick Arts Publishing Limited   +44 (0)1403 256941

Published October 2017

A CIP catalogue record for this book is available at the British Library.

ISBN 978-1-84886-282-1

www.maverickbooks.co.uk